X Green, Sara, 1964-
362.4048 Service dogs BER
3
GRE 4/2015

DOGS TO THE RESCUE!
SERVICE DOGS

By Sara Green

BELLWETHER MEDIA • MINNEAPOLIS, MN

Jump into the cockpit and take flight with *Pilot books*. Your journey will take you on high-energy adventures as you learn about all that is wild, weird, fascinating, and fun!

This edition first published in 2014 by Bellwether Media, Inc.

No part of this publication may be reproduced in whole or in part without written permission of the publisher. For information regarding permission, write to Bellwether Media, Inc., Attention: Permissions Department, 5357 Penn Avenue South, Minneapolis, MN 55419.

Library of Congress Cataloging-in-Publication Data

Green, Sara, 1964-
 Service dogs / by Sara Green.
    pages cm. – (Pilot: Dogs to the rescue!)
 Summary: "Engaging images accompany information about service dogs. The combination of high-interest subject matter and narrative text is intended for students in grades 3 through 7"– Provided by publisher.
 Includes bibliographical references and index.
 ISBN 978-1-60014-958-0 (hardcover : alk. paper)
 1. Service dogs–Juvenile literature. 2. Working dogs–Juvenile literature. I. Title.
 HV1569.6.G74 2014
 362.4'0483–dc23
                                                            2013008932

Text copyright © 2014 by Bellwether Media, Inc. PILOT and associated logos are trademarks and/or registered trademarks of Bellwether Media, Inc. SCHOLASTIC, CHILDREN'S PRESS, and associated logos are trademarks and/or registered trademarks of Scholastic Inc.

Printed in the United States of America, North Mankato, MN.

TABLE OF CONTENTS

A Service Dog Named Trooper 4

Skilled Helpers 6

Training to Serve 14

Changing Lives Every Day 18

Endal: A Service Dog Hero 20

Glossary 22

To Learn More 23

Index 24

A SERVICE DOG NAMED TROOPER

Kyle Smith has **post-polio syndrome**. This condition makes his arms and legs weak, and he tires easily. As a result, he uses a wheelchair to move around. Kyle's yellow Labrador Retriever, Trooper, helps him stay independent. Trooper is a highly trained service dog that keeps close to Kyle's side.

When Kyle wants a snack, Trooper tugs on a strap to open the refrigerator door. When things fall on the floor, Trooper picks them up and drops them in Kyle's hands. Trooper also uses his nose to push buttons to open doors for Kyle. Trooper is the best tail-wagging helper Kyle could ask for!

SKILLED HELPERS

People with **disabilities** want to live independent lives. Service dogs make this possible for them. These specially trained dogs live with their partners and help with daily needs around the house. They also help their partners in public places. The law allows service dogs to go anywhere their partners go. They accompany their partners to work and school. They are allowed in restaurants, movie theaters, grocery stores, and malls. Service dogs even travel with their partners on buses, trains, and subways. When service dogs fly on planes, they sit in the cabin at their partner's feet.

The most common service dog breeds are the Golden Retriever and Labrador Retriever. They are known for their intelligence and gentle nature. Many other breeds, both large and small, are also used for service work. No matter the breed, service dogs must be smart, friendly, and loyal. They also must be eager to work!

The First Service Dog

A small black Labrador and Golden Retriever mix named Abdul made history in the mid-1970s. He became the first service dog to partner with a physically disabled person. Abdul was also the first service dog to visit Disneyland!

Breeds Of Service Dogs

Golden Retriever

Labrador Retriever

Great Dane

Many service dogs assist people who use wheelchairs because of physical disabilities. Their main job is to help with **mobility**. The service dogs go on outings with their partners to help them navigate public places with ease. The dogs pull the wheelchairs up ramps, open doors, and push elevator buttons. At home, the dogs retrieve dropped items and flip light switches on and off. They open cabinets and drawers. Some dogs even pull off their partner's shoes, socks, and other clothing to help them undress.

Profile: Golden Retriever

Intelligence
The Golden Retriever is the fourth smartest dog breed. The dog learns and obeys new commands almost immediately.

Size
Height: 20 to 24 inches (51 to 61 centimeters)

Weight: 55 to 80 pounds (25 to 36 kilograms)

Characteristics
The Golden Retriever is friendly, loyal, and eager to please. The breed's early use as a hunting dog makes it natural for the dog to retrieve objects for its owner.

People who need assistance to stand or walk can use service dogs to help them balance. The dogs, often Great Danes, wear special **harnesses** that are easy to grip. They help their partners walk, navigate stairs, and stand from chairs.

Many people have disabilities that are not visible. They also use service dogs. Hearing dogs are trained to alert people with hearing **impairments**. These dogs recognize when someone calls their partner's name. They nudge their partner to alert them. They also respond to sounds such as smoke alarms, microwave ovens, and alarm clocks. They let their partner know when the doorbell or phone rings. They even respond to a baby's cry.

Seizure alert dogs help people who have **epilepsy** and similar conditions. A seizure dog barks when it senses its partner is about to have a seizure. This gives the partner time to get in a safe place or call for help before the seizure begins.

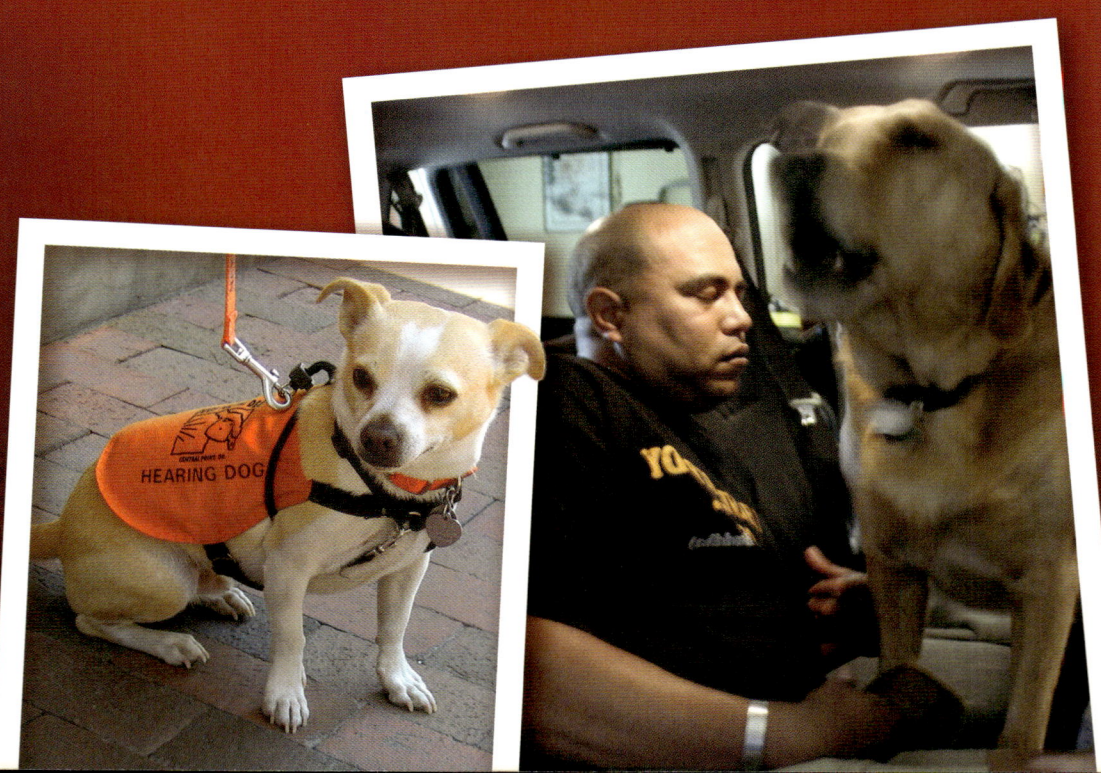

Guide Dogs

Guide dogs are another type of service dog. They help people who are blind or nearly blind. These dogs are trained to guide their owners safely from one place to another.

Service dogs also assist people with severe mental health illnesses. These illnesses include depression and **post-traumatic stress disorder**. Mental health service dogs provide emotional support to people. People with mental health illnesses feel more secure when they have a service dog at their side. The dogs comfort their partners during panic attacks. They wake their partners from nightmares and help them feel confident in crowds. Some dogs even remind their partners to take their medications!

Dog at Work

Service dogs at work usually wear special vests. When the dogs wear these vests, they need to stay focused on their partners. For this reason, people must always ask for permission to pet a service dog.

TRAINING TO SERVE

Many service dogs are trained at service dog training centers. Training begins when service dogs are puppies. The pups live at home with **puppy raisers**. These individuals or families are chosen by the training center. Puppies live with their raisers in a safe, loving home for six months to a year.

The raisers teach the pups basic manners and **obedience skills**. They also **socialize** the puppies to different people and situations. The puppies wear vests that identify them as service dogs in training. They accompany their raisers wherever they go. This way, the puppies learn to be comfortable around strangers and children. They get used to loud noises, shopping carts, wheelchairs, and other things that might surprise a dog in public. Puppy raisers help dogs become confident and friendly in all situations.

After they have mastered basic skills, the dogs move in with trainers. This training usually takes 6 months or more, depending on how much the dog needs to learn. Trainers teach the dogs the special skills they will use to help their partners. For example, mobility service dogs learn to pull straps with their mouths. This allows them to open refrigerators and cupboards. They learn to use their paws to press buttons to open automatic doors and turn on lamps. Many even learn how to dial 911 on a telephone.

Service dogs take a test at the end of their training program. They must prove that they can follow all of the trainer's commands. They also must behave well in public to pass the test. If a dog passes, it receives a badge and **certification** as a service dog. Then the dog is ready to be placed with a partner.

CHANGING LIVES EVERY DAY

People with disabilities face many struggles. Sometimes they feel discouraged, sad, or lonely. Strangers may feel uncomfortable around people with disabilities. They do not know how to act or what to say. Service dogs can help. They take attention away from the disability. This makes it easier for others to approach the pair. People can show interest in the service dog and ask questions. Many people find new friends this way.

Service dogs also boost their partners' moods. Caring for a dog helps a person feel responsible and positive. At work or at play, these faithful companions bring joy to many people's lives!

ENDAL: A SERVICE DOG HERO

In 1991, a British Navy officer named Allen Parton suffered a severe head injury in war. As a result, he lost much of his memory and could not speak for many years. He also lost the use of both legs and needed to use a wheelchair. Allen often felt like staying in bed all day. Then he was partnered with Endal, a very special service dog.

Endal was a Labrador Retriever. He understood more than 100 verbal commands and hand signals. His many skills included loading the washing machine and pulling items from grocery store shelves. He was the first dog to learn how to put a cash card into a cash machine. He could also remove the card and return it to Allen's wallet. Endal helped make Allen's life very happy. He also helped other people. Endal visited sick children and inspired people to care about animals. He received many awards for his outstanding achievements. Endal died in 2009, but he will always be remembered as a service dog hero.

GLOSSARY

certification—official recognition that a dog has mastered specific job skills

disabilities—physical or mental conditions that limit a person's abilities

epilepsy—a brain condition that causes people to have seizures

harnesses—straps that fit around dogs' shoulders and chests

impairments—reduced abilities

mobility—the ability to move around

obedience skills—skills that include sit, stay, come, and down

post-polio syndrome—a condition that causes people to have severe muscle weakness and pain that gets worse over time

post-traumatic stress disorder—severe anxiety that occurs after a person experiences a terrifying event

puppy raisers—volunteers who care for puppies that will grow up to be guide dogs and service dogs

seizure—a loss of body control caused by a burst of electrical activity in the brain

socialize—to teach dogs to have good manners in all kinds of situations

TO LEARN MORE

AT THE LIBRARY
Bozzo, Linda. *Service Dog Heroes*. Berkeley Heights, N.J.: Bailey Books/Enslow, 2011.

Hoffman, Mary Ann. *Helping Dogs*. New York, N.Y.: Gareth Stevens Pub., 2011.

Tagliaferro, Linda. *Service Dogs*. New York, N.Y.: Bearport Pub., 2005.

ON THE WEB
Learning more about service dogs is as easy as 1, 2, 3.

1. Go to www.factsurfer.com.

2. Enter "service dogs" into the search box.

3. Click the "Surf" button and you will see a list of related Web sites.

With factsurfer.com, finding more information is just a click away.

INDEX

Abdul, 7
breeds, 6, 7, 9
certification, 17
characteristics, 6, 9, 14
emotional support, 13, 18, 19, 21
Endal, 20, 21
Golden Retriever 6, 7, 9
Great Dane, 7, 9
guide dogs, 11
harnesses, 9
hearing dogs, 10
history, 7, 20, 21
Labrador Retriever, 4, 6, 7, 21
laws, 6
mental health service dogs, 13
mobility dogs, 8, 9, 16
obedience skills, 14

Parton, Allen, 20, 21
physical disabilities, 4, 7, 8, 9
post-polio syndrome, 4
post-traumatic stress disorder, 13
public places, 6, 8, 14, 17
puppy raisers, 14
seizure alert dogs, 10
skills, 4, 8, 9, 10, 11, 13, 14, 16, 21
socialization, 14
training, 14, 16, 17
vests, 13, 14
wheelchairs, 4, 8, 14, 20

The images in this book are reproduced through the courtesy of: KariDesign, front cover; J. De Meester/ GlowImages, front cover, pp. 6-7, 8; Huntstock/ GlowImages, pp. 4, 5; EpicStockMedia, p. 7 (top); AnetaPics, p. 7 (middle & bottom); Linn Currie, p. 9; Jeroen van den Broek, pp. 10-11; Steve Shoup, p. 10 (left); Maisonneuve Jacqulyn/ SIPA/ Newscom, p. 10 (right); age fotostock/ SuperStock, p. 12; chapin31, p. 13; Pablo Alcaca/ AP Images, pp. 14-15; Hans Gutknecht/ ZUMA Press/ Newscom, p. 16; David Stephenson/ ZUMA Press/ Newscom, p. 17; iofoto, p. 18; Rick Wilking/ Newscom, p. 19; Mike Hollist / Associated Newspapers / Rex Features/ Alamy, pp. 20 (left), 21; Jim Watson/ AP Photo/ Getty Images/ Newscom, p. 20 (right).